Flowering

Love is foe, Volume 1

KERNAN

Published by KERNAN, 2023.

While every precaution has been taken in the preparation of this book, the publisher assumes no responsibility for errors or omissions, or for damages resulting from the use of the information contained herein.

FLOWERING

First edition. September 2, 2023.

Copyright © 2023 KERNAN.

ISBN: 979-8215651636

Written by KERNAN.

Flowering

Chapter 1-the beginning

A life of pain and endless strife,
With anger burning deep inside,
The urge for vengeance takes hold,
Fueled by a need that won't subside.
The fire of revenge consumes the soul,
Turning love and light to coal,
The darkness grows, the heart goes cold,
And the need to right the wrongs takes hold.
The quest for justice becomes an obsession,
With every move fueled by aggression,
The line between right and wrong blurred,
As the need for revenge becomes assured.
But as the journey goes on,
The lines begin to blur,
Between revenge and redemption,
And what was once so pure.
No longer do the wounds of the past,
Hold their firm and painful grasp,
For redemption emerges to the fore,
And a new path begins to carve.
Where anger once did reign,
A new light begins to shine,
A path towards new hope and love,
A chance for a fresh start to climb.
The message in this tale lies within,
The nature of revenge and the path to redemption,
A journey that lies within oneself,
A lesson learned and a new beginning commenced.
2. In the corner of my mind, there sits a trolley old,
From memories that I cherish, its significance I hold,

It held so many bags, each one was unique,
Tattered and battered, but carrying stories beneath.
The very sight of them would bring a smile to my face,
Standing there, like soldiers, with poise and grace,
They held the joy and laughter, and the anguish and grief,
Each piece was an extension, of the owner and their belief.
But as time went by, I saw it slowly rotting away,
The once-beautiful colours, now faded and gray,
The happy memories once contained within,
Were now overshadowed, by the rust and metallic din.
The trolley lay there unattended, as if no longer loved,
Discarded and forgotten, like a hand missing a glove,
As I stand there gazing, lost in deep thought,
I realise that the trolley is like life, slowly rotting and fraught.
But just like the memories once contained within,
Life still holds its beauty, despite all the din and din,
So let us cherish every moment with love and grace,
And like the trolley of old, have stories to tell with pride and pace.
3. The winds of this island are mighty and fierce,
They howl and they screech, making all quiver in fear.
The residents know that the wind is no friend,
It shows its power and abuse again and again.
But these island dwellers are not ones to cower,
Their spirits are strong, they have a lot of power.
They stand up to the wind, they battle it hard,
Their kind is resilient, their courage unmarred.
As the wind pushes against them, they push back,
Their determination never slack.
They know that the wind must be tamed,
Or else everything they hold dear will be maimed.
The people of this island are brave and proud,
Their will to survive forever endowed.

From generation to generation, they've passed on,
The knowledge of how to brave the wind and its song.
So the winds may still howl and scream,
But these island dwellers won't be deemed.
Their strength and resilience will always endure,
Their kind will forever stay strong and pure.

4. Amidst the storm, the waves doth rise
   With winds that howl and twist the skies
A tempest brews, so mighty and big
Whose force the ocean does upheave and jig
A boat bobs and weaves upon the waves
Its captain stares back at memories engraves
Of a life lived full, of love and adventure
But now his fate lies in the storm's denture
For the howling winds and raging sea
Are far too strong for the boat to flee
And as the vessel is tossed and turned
The captain's memories within him burned
Of love and laughter, of heartbreak and pain
Of moments cherished, now forever stained
With the knowledge that his time is nigh
And the storm will soon make him say goodbye
Yet as the storm rages on and on
The captain feels a calmness dawn
For he knows that his soul will soon be free
And that his memories will always be
A comfort in the midst of the storm
A light that shines, bright and warm
Guiding him towards his final rest
And granting him eternal peace and rest.
5. The voltra crackles, sparking with bright light
Revealing a conflict, an awful sight:
Favoritism reigns, one class is exalted
While the others are left feeling assaulted.
The pain and suffering of those cast out
Is evident, clear, there is no doubt

The euphoria of the chosen is palpable, too
As they revel in their elevated view.
But there is a deeper struggle at play
One that cannot be seen from afar away.
Injustice reigns, and it cuts like a knife
As one group thrives while another struggles for life.
So let us use this voltra's bright light
To reveal a solution, and set things right.
For fairness and justice must be our guide
To bridge the gap and let all rise together, side by side.
6. The sky grows dark, a storm is near,
But yet it seems so far from here.
The air is tight, so heavy, too,
With conflicting interests that ensue.
Obsession fights with doubt and fear,
Like lightning strikes, so sharp and clear.
The winds of change begin to blow,
And soon the storm will start to grow.
A battle rages in the sky,
As dark clouds gather, passing by.
The thunder roars, the rain pours down,
The lightning bolts, they all surround.
But here below, we simply wait,
And hope the storm will dissipate.
For even though the air's so tight,
We're not yet ready for the fight.
We'll weather out the coming storm,
And soon the skies will start to warm.
Then we'll look back and see with glee,
The storm that once was, now set free.

7. In the depths of my mind
There are memories intertwined.
A childhood of turmoil and strife,
Haunts me still, even in adult life.
The pain and hurt that I endured,
Has left me feeling so unsure.
But with time, I've learned to cope,
And now I choose to have hope.
The memories can come rushing back,
A wave of darkness and attack.
But I am not the same as before,
I have strength now, and so much more.
My influence has grown with time,
Giving me power to confront the crime.
The abuser that once held me down,
Can no longer keep me bound.
I am strong, I am free,
No longer held captive by the past you see.
The memories may still linger,
But I am the one in control, the bringer.
Bringer of hope, of light and of peace,
My past may have been troubled, but it will not cease.
I am the one who decides my fate,
And with that power, I will not be late.
To flourish, to thrive, and to grow,
Is what my potential has come to show.
And so, I stand here today,
A survivor, not a victim, come what may.
8. In the eye of the beholder,
Lies a beauty that's unique,

But what happens when we're older,
And our insecurities make us weak?
We fight ourselves mentally,
Comparing to what we see,
But beauty is not just external,
It's in our heart, and it's in our deeds.
For when we see ourselves, we're critical,
Finding fault in every flaw,
But it's our imperfections that make us beautiful,
And help us grow after we fall.
It's in the moments of struggle,
That we find our strength and grace,
And see that the beauty that's within us,
Can shine through the darkest of days.
So let us embrace the bittersweet,
And see ourselves with kinder eyes,
For the beauty that we hold inside,
Is what truly illuminates our lives.

9. Her beauty, oh, how it shines,
    A sight that takes my breath away,
Age, a mere number, just a line,
With time, her allure never fades.
Her smile, a ray of sunshine,
Radiant as it was in her youth,
Her eyes, like jewels, always divine,
A beauty that's truly never aloof.
For though age may take its toll,
And wrinkles may set in,
It's the depth of the soul,
That truly makes beauty begin.
For as the years go on, and life progresses,
Our beauty is not found in our youth,
But in the wisdom and experiences,
That shape us, and reveal a deeper truth.
So let us not be fearful of the years,
Or what time may bring,
For with age, we gain a beauty,
That is truly an everlasting thing.
10. In front of the mirror, I stand and gaze
At the lines that cross my aging face
As time passes by, so much has changed
Chasing dreams and memories arranged
My once youthful eyes, with a twinkle so bright
Now tired, dull, and fading from sight
Though my bus of life has moved ahead
The past has left its mark on my head
I can see the sunshine and dreams come alive
But darkness sometimes clouds my eyes

The road can be rough, the journey long
And the memories that surface can be so wrong
My youthful spirit may no longer be around
Buried deep in the past, it can't be found
The dreams that once kept me alive
Now seem crushed, with struggle to revive
But I refuse to be left behind
I'll keep going, keep pushing through time
The bus may bend and sway with age
But still, it moves forward, frame by frame
The symbol of hope, the bus of life
Is more than just an image in sight
It's a reminder to stay on course
And keep moving forward, with willful force
The past may have scars that remain
But the future is a blank slate, free and plain
So I'll keep my feet on the ground
And keep driving my bus, with hopes abound
For even though the mirror can be tough to view
I'll embrace what it reflects; the things that are true
And keep pressing forward to the end
With my bus as my steadfast friend.
11.
Hate boils within like wildfire,
It consumes, it devours, it perspires.
The distant bus seems miles away,
As I'm consumed by a corrupting desire.
Money and fame, they are all-consuming,
They make us forget the simple things.
We forget love, we forget joy,
And in its place, hatred and death we bring.
The bus carries people to their destinations,

But they are blind to their own damnation.
Corrupted by wealth and status,
Their souls drowned in eternal damnation.
As I watch the bus fade away,
I'm left with the consequence of their actions.
The world is filled with death and hate,
Thanks to their greed and wicked attractions.
So I stand here, consumed by loathing,
Hoping that one day they will see.
That money and fame are fleeting pleasures,
And true happiness lies in simplicity.
12. the road ahead I see a bus so grand,
A shining symbol of success and demand.
It seems so far away, in the distant land,
But sure enough, it's moving closer, oh so grand.
As the bus approaches, my heart starts to race,
I feel my feet lift up from their earthly place.
My mind starts to drift, I'm lost in the grace
Of the success this bus promises, I could taste.
But reality fades as I board the bus,
My senses overwhelmed by this newfound fuss.
I'm lost in the dream, nothing can discuss,
The pull towards success, without any fuss.
So hold on tight, as you board this bus of glory,
And let success be the end of your story.
Drift away into the land of the most holy,
And achieve the greatest success, ever so boldly.

13. Love is a rose, so beautiful and bright,
A symbol of beauty that shines so right,
Its fragrance so sweet, it captures your heart,
And fills you up right from the very start.
But beauty can hide a much darker truth,
Inside the petals, there's more than youth,
The thorns that prick as you reach for the rose,
Are like a warning that nobody knows.
For inside of us lies a different story,
Full of sorrow, pain, and not much glory,
Our beauty shines out, but it's not the whole,
For the essence of love comes from the soul.
And when the petals fall, and death takes hold,
Our true colors are revealed, black as coal,
The love that once bloomed now withers and dies,
And all that's left is brokenhearted sighs.
So don't be fooled by the beauty outside,
For it's what's within that counts, not just pride,
For the essence of love is truly pure,
And lasts forever, of that you can be sure.
14. Life, a precious and fleeting gift,
Filled with moments we hold and uplift.
Each breath we take, a treasure to embrace,
An experience to cherish, no time to waste.
Loss, a pain that slices through the soul,
Leaves us feeling empty, a gaping hole.
But in the midst of heartbreak and despair,
We find strength and love, to bear and repair.
The beauty of life is the love we share,
That blooms and blossoms, beyond compare.

The memories we make with one another,
A bond that lasts, beyond time's cover.
Yet even in moments, life can feel unjust,
Hatred and cruelty, towards us thrust.
The pain we feel, when met with disgust,
Can leave us reeling, our spirits crushed.
But in the face of animosity and spite,
We choose to stand, with all our might.
For deep within, we know the truth,
That love conquers hate, it's absolute proof.
And so, we live life, with our hearts open,
Loving and caring, with every emotion.
For in the end, it's not how long we live,
But how much love we give, that helps us thrive.
Life is beautiful, yet fragile and fleeting,
Filled with both sorrows and joyful greetings.
We must embrace it all, with open arms,
Including loss, hatred, and life's harms.
For the deepest meaning of life, we discover,
Is to live and love, and with grace recover.
And when we leave this earth, we can rest,
Knowing our lives were loved, and truly blessed.
15. Life, oh life, a beauty to behold,
A myriad of colors, memories, untold.
With every step, a rollercoaster ride,
Empowering, astounding, takes you on a ride.
Breathtaking moments that make your heart swell,
Joyful laughter, and stories to tell.
The warmth of the sun and the kiss of the breeze
A kiss so warm it brings you to your knees.
Yet pain, oh pain, that lurks within,
Hurtful memories, and devastating sins.

Emotions so raw, it's hard not to sink,
Just a glimmer of hope makes you think.
But then the light of hope shines so bright
That even in the darkness, it brings delight.
In the face of adversity, we grow strong
And keep moving forward, where we belong.
Although life can be unforgiving and harsh at times,
The beauty it holds makes us find the rhymes.
A mix of joy and sorrow, in equal measure we see
The yin and yang of life, an inevitable decree.
So let us cherish and live life with glee
The highs and lows, a necessary guarantee.
Embrace the beauty and tough times with grace,
For life's lessons are what makes us a human race.

16. In the land of plenty and excess,
Exists a world so poor and oppressed,
A social poverty that's hard to confess,
Where survival is just a constant test.
Post code wars reign supreme,
And street smarts are the only thing,
In some neighbourhoods it's just a dream,
To live in peace and not feel the sting.
Gangs of youth roam the streets,
With no real purpose or direction,
Hurt and anger is all they meet,
In a constant state of tension.
Social status reigns supreme,
And stereotypes become the norm,
Where people's worth is just a dream,
In a world that's so morally deformed.
But unconditional love has the power,
To break down the barriers and walls,
To help the broken find their flower,
And stand tall as society crawls.
So let's reach out and lend a hand,
To those in need and under the gun,
To help them break free from this land,
And rise to a new challenge just begun.
For social poverty and the post code wars,
Are not set in stone or hard to crack,
Let's work together, let's open new doors,
And ensure the future is never too black.
17. Controlling and conflicting, two sides within
That battle it out, a constant din

One seeks dominance over every thought
The other challenges, in search of what's sought
Control, a necessary tool for the mind
To keep thoughts in check, to always find
A way forward, without getting lost
To reach the destination, at any cost
But conflict too, has its own value
For it challenges the status quo, anew
To question what we know, and what we believe
And to never stop, until we achieve
Balance is key, between these two states
To control when needed, but also create
Conflict when necessary, to push us ahead
To achieve our goals, without losing our head
So embrace both sides, for what they are worth
And learn to navigate, the highs and the dearths
With control and conflict, both on your side
You'll achieve all your dreams, and so much more besides.
18. Good and evil battle on,
A struggle that lasts until dawn;
Both sides vying for control,
The fate of humanity their goal.
The darkness creeps in like a thief,
Stealing belongingness and our belief;
It thrives on pain and suffering,
While the light battles for a belonging.
Goodness offers love and hope,
Its light a way to help those who cope;
It seeks to unite and bring peace,
Making sure all hatred will cease.
The bonds that they create,
Determines who will end up in the gates;

Goodness offers the warmth of belonging,
The evil creates things that are so wrong.
So hold on tight to the light,
And let the hope be shining bright;
For we are all in this fight,
Together, united, with hearts alight.
19. A constant feeling of failure,
haunts my every thought,
the weight of society's standards,
seems to be all for naught.
I try to fit into the mold,
but always fall apart,
my flaws and imperfections,
tearing me right from the start.
The endless list of expectations,
seems to never end,
and in this endless cycle,
I can never seem to blend.
I try to hide my feelings,
beneath a well-crafted veneer,
but the pressure of society,
causes my mental health to veer.
I feel like a failure,
with each and every breath,
the expectations of success,
weighing down like a heavy death.
Yet should I cease to try,
or go my own way,
I'm met with disapproval,
and judgment each day.
The world is like a river,
flowing on its own,

but refusing to comply,
can leave us all alone.
Is it better to be true to oneself,
even if it means being alone?
Or is it better to comply,
and let our true selves remain unknown?
Perhaps the answer lies in between,
balancing expectation and desire,
seeking to find a way,
to build our own futures higher.
So let us embrace our failures,
let us learn from each mistake,
for it is only in the journey,
that we can truly make.
And though the world may judge us,
and our failures may seem to define,
we must remember that success,
comes with the strength to always try.

20.

Oh, the weight of sinning and neglect,
A burden heavy, hard to correct,
The heart sinks deep into despair,
And sin's embrace becomes a snare.
Neglect, a subtle foe it seems,
A creeping vine that saps the dreams,
A thousand tasks left undone,
That builds up and bears no fun.
The humdrum life of day to day,
With no time for rest or play,
Pushing back what should be done,
Until there's nowhere else to run.
And so the guilt begins to grow,
A toxic seed that learns to sow,
The seeds of sin take root and sprout,
And every scan repeats the doubt.
The little routines of life now fade,
And all that's left is shame and trade,
And burdens bear down one by one,
As restitution can't be won.
The regrets and guilt of what's been done,
The wounds inflicted by neglect and fun,
But even so it's not too late,
To turn around and change our fate.
Let's cast away the sins of old,
And clear the path to hearts made bold,
With each step forward as we learn,
New life and hope will us turn.
So, let's shake off the chains of neglect,
And leave the sinning to its neglect,

For life's too short to live with pain,
And joy can still thrive once again.
21. The depths of sadness penetrate so deep
My soul is heavy with the weight I keep
Grief and loss consume me whole
And depression takes its toll
I try to rise above my pain
But sorrow pulls me down again
The memories and tears persist
An unending cycle that cannot be dismissed
The world around me moves along
But I am trapped in this mournful song
I long to feel joy and laughter once more
But the darkness lingers, evermore
Each day is a struggle to get through
My heart a heavy burden it must bear, too
The light that once shone brightly within
Has dimmed, leaving only darkness and sin
I try to cling to hope and faith
But depression tells me it's too late
The weight of sadness too heavy to bear
Leaves me unable to do more than stare
The tears fall freely, a constant stream
As I try to live through this dark dream
My heart aches for the love and life I've lost
But all I feel now is the cost
Grief and sadness, sorrow and pain
Depression's grip refuses to wane
But I will not give up this fight
To find my way back to the light
I'll reach out for help and embrace
The love and support around my space

Perhaps one day, the darkness will depart
And light will once again fill my heart.
22. In the twilight of the years,
As the sun sets and disappears,
We often look back and reflect,
On the moments that we've collected.
We remember laughter and love,
The joys that made our hearts soar above,
But there is also sadness and pain,
Moments we wish we could abstain.
And as we sit and reminisce,
We can't help but feel something amiss,
A longing for what we once had,
A wish to be young once more, not sad.
We miss the vigor of youth,
The energy, the unblemished truth,
The unbridled passion to explore,
The feeling of being able to soar.
We long for the carefree days,
The lack of worries, the simple ways,
The feeling that nothing could stop,
Us from reaching the mountaintop.
But with age comes a different kind of grace,
A sense of wisdom that comes with pace,
A deeper understanding of oneself,
An appreciation of life's true wealth.
And while we may wish to be young again,
We should never forget what we've attained,
The lessons learned, the memories shared,
The compassion and kindness that we've declared.
For in our twilight years,
We can offer something that's rare,

Our own unique brand of empathy,
To help those who are struggling to see.
So let us not yearn for youth too long,
But instead, let us sing our life's song,
With the compassion that comes with age,
Guiding others through life's oft-difficult stage.

Chapter 8- shadows in my mind

23. In shadows deep, a battle rages on
      Between the virtues of hope and failure's spawn
Within us both, they struggle for control
A endless cycle of triumph and toll
Hope rises high, its light shining bright
A beacon of promise, a guiding light
But as failure creeps in, doubts start to grow
A helpless feeling, like we'll never know
Which path to choose, which way to turn
The battle rages on, and our hearts burn
Yet we stand firm, our will unbroken
With courage and strength, our spirits awoken
For in this fight, we are not alone
Others have battled, and seeds have been sown
Of a brighter future, free of despair
If we hold on tight and continue to care
So let us choose, to fight with our might
Against the darkness, until it's out of sight
For in the end, it's often the case
That hope and perseverance win the race.
24. In the depths of despair, you once did reside,
But hope was calling, you could not hide.
With a newfound determination to rise to your best,
You stepped forward, and put yourself to the test.
Your journey was rocky, full of ups and downs,
But you refused to let yourself fall to the ground.
Anxiety and depression tried to hold you back,
But you learned to overcome, and stay on track.
You found that it was okay to ask for a hand,
And with each day, you grew to understand.

That your struggles and pain were not in vain,
For they helped shape you, and made you gain.
Your hope continued to burn, like a shining light,
As you fought, and never gave up the fight.
You rose above your fears, and soared higher still,
Refusing to be confined, by depression's will.
So, if you find yourself in a dark place,
Remember that there's still hope, to embrace.
You can become the best version of yourself,
By never giving up, on the journey of mental health.
25.
As a child, we start out so small,
Learning about the world, taking it all,
With curiosity in our eyes,
We explore and discover, to our surprise.
As we grow, our troubles increase,
Challenges arise that never seem to cease,
We search for guidance, a light in the dark,
A pathway to lead us, to make a new start.
Hope flickers inside, a small flame,
Guiding us through life's changing game,
Through twists and turns, we learn to cope,
Building character, resilience and hope.
We forge ahead, with every step we take,
Knowing that each choice we make,
Will shape our lives, and lead us on,
To becoming the best version, of who we really are.
Although the journey may be long,
And times of struggle may come along,
The path of hope, will help us to see,
That with faith and perseverance, we can truly be free.
So let us all continue to grow,

And find the strength, to let hope flow,
For in the end, it will be clear to see,
That we have become, the person we were meant to be.
26. A dream
Oh, dreamer, do not be afraid
To chase the dreams that you have made
For there is nothing in this life
More beautiful than your own light
Though others may try to dissuade
And hardships may come in your way
Stay true to what you know is right
And never lose your will to fight
For dreams can take you to new heights
And fill your life with wondrous sights
So trust within your heart and soul
And let your dreams take full control
Let go of fear and doubt and strife
And choose to live this precious life
With passion, hope, and love in sight
Pursue your dreams, with all your might
For in the end, it's what we do
That makes a life that's bright and true
So take a leap and dare to be
The person that you long to see
And if you ever start to stray
Just trust in yourself, come what may
For dreams have power, beyond compare
And will always lead you, to where
You're meant to be, your destiny
Trust in your dreams, and you will see
The magic that they will unfold
In ways that you will never know

27. Gap of love
In my heart, there's a void, a painful gap
The memory of you, it makes me sad
But I know that time won't ever stop
And the love we shared, it can never end
I've had my doubts, I've lost my way
My heart was broken, but that was yesterday
I had to learn to trust, to love again
And with every step, I regained my strength
Now I stand here, with a smile so bright
I've found my purpose, my dream in sight
And though you're gone, I know you're proud
Of all I've done, of all I'll become
For every loss, there's a gain
And though my heart will never be the same
I'll cherish the memories, and hold them dear
As I continue on, with you always near
So here's to love, and here's to life
Here's to all the struggles and the strife
For in the end, we'll find our way
And love will guide us, every day.
28. A hill
In search of hope and happiness,
We climb the hills with all our might,
Striving hard to find our true selves,
And embrace our souls with all our light.
The climb seems long and never-ending,
With stumbling blocks along the way,
But with unwavering determination,
We move forward day by day.
As we ascend up that mountain high,
We realize our strength and grit,

That we have the power to conquer all,
And light the fire that never quits.
And when we reach the peak at last,
Our hearts filled with love and bliss,
We finally see our true selves,
And embrace the joy we cannot miss.
So let us climb that hill with pride,
And trust in our own abilities,
With hope and happiness on our side,
We'll find ourselves and be free.
29. The path of light
The light follows you at every turn,
A faithful companion that you can discern,
It brightens the way and lights up the night,
Guiding you till the path is in sight.
As you walk through the twists and the bends,
The light stays with you till the very end,
It shows you the way, it leads you on,
Till you reach your destination, your journey done.
But sometimes the light can be deceiving,
And lead you astray without your knowing,
It can lure you towards a path unknown,
Towards a place where you feel all alone.
And so you wander in the dark and the cold,
Till you see the path of exile unfold,
But fear not, my friend, for the light still shines,
Guiding you towards better times.
So keep your head up, keep moving ahead,
For the light will show you the way instead,
And though the road may be uncertain and wild,
The light will follow you like a faithful child
30. In the depths of despair,

The world seems bleak and bare
With no light to guide the way
It's easy to lose faith and stray
But hope is a tiny flame
That flickers despite the shame
It lifts us up and carries us through
Giving us the strength to start anew
With every sunrise comes a chance
To break free from the devil's dance
To spread wings and take to the sky
Leaving the pain and sorrow behind
Yet hope can also be deceiving
A false sense of comfort, fleeting
For the flame that once burned bright
Can be extinguished in the night
Thus, we must learn to bear
The burden of a world unfair
Find strength in the darkness too
And never lose sight of what is true
For hope and despair are two sides
Of the same coin that fate decides
A reminder that life is but a cycle
Of ups and downs, moments of spectacle
So when hope wanes and despair looms
Remember that they're two parts of one room
For every end marks a new beginning
And every loss a chance for winning.

31. Greatness in the eye

In life we search for greatness,
A sense of purpose and pure elation,
But sometimes the path is winding,
And met with disappointment and frustration.

We strive for success and achievement,
A life full of triumph and pride,
But failure can creep up and catch us,
And make us feel like we're shattered inside.
But failures are lessons we must accept,
To learn and grow towards our goal,
With each setback we gain wisdom,
And become stronger in heart and soul.
So don't fear the possibility of defeat,
Embrace it as a chance to persevere,
For greatness lies in the willingness to try,
And the resilience to overcome fear.
Have hope, my friend, and keep moving,
Through defeats and failures, stand tall,
For in the face of adversity and challenge,
We can rise and achieve, after all.

32. In life's journey, we all seek
A soul to call our own
A companion to share our heart
A love that will be shown
Amidst the chaos and the noise
I found my one true light
My heart skipped a beat and knew
This love felt just so right
With each passing moment
My love grows more each day
Together we will face the world
Our hearts beating as one, come what may
With love and affection, we embrace
Each other's hopes and dreams
Our hearts full of laughter
And love that forever beams
In each other's arms we find peace
A love that will never wane
Together we walk life's path
With each other always to remain
My heart is filled with gratitude
As I hold you close to me
The one I've searched for all my life
My love, my destiny..

33. A march
Memories flood my mind,
Of soldiers marching in a line,
Their weapons tight in their grip,
Marching towards a fateful trip.
The clanging of metal on metal,

Echoes through the air like a kettle,
The sound of boots hitting the ground,
As they march towards an enemy unbound.
The blood drips from the palace walls,
As the sound of war echoes in the halls,
A scene that's too gruesome to bear,
As the soldiers fight with a deadly stare.
The memory of war, so vivid and real,
Is something that one can never conceal,
It's etched deeply into the mind,
A haunting reminder of another kind.
As I close my eyes, I can hear
The sounds of war still ringing clear,
A stark reminder of what it was,
To march into battle, fighting for a cause.
But as the memories come and go,
I'm safe in my home without a foe,
A luxury that I can't help but be grateful for,
As I remember the horrors of war.

34. A song

A melody, a tune, a song so sweet,
Echoes through the miles, around our feet.
But don't be fooled by the sound so mild,
For on the other side, it's guns and roses and blood, wild.
The rhythm flows like a river so vast,
As we approach the land where shadows are cast.
The beat picks up, the tempo seems to rise,
But the closer we get, the more danger lies.
The lyrics tell a tale of love and desire,
But in this place, passion leads to gunfire.
The guitar riffs cut through the air like knives,
And the drums beat like hearts struggling to survive.

The chorus repeats, a refrain so clear,
But the screams in the distance make it hard to hear.
The music's power can't erase the pain,
For in this land it's all strife, no gain.
So let us tread carefully, and listen close,
For this song has a message, it's not just a dose,
Of entertainment, but a warning of what's true,
On the other side, where guns and roses bloom anew.
35.
Roses bloom and hills are alive
The footprint of a man who once thrived
Memories of his life, now just a trace
As nature claims back its rightful space
The fragrance of roses fills the air
A gentle reminder of the man who once cared
For the beauty that bloomed over the hills
And the stories that he would always tell.
His footprints still remain deep in the earth
A reminder of his life and his worth
And though he may not be here anymore
His spirit lives on in the rose's allure.
The roses bloom and the hills sing
Of a life that once was, and everything
The beauty that this land still holds
And the stories remain, to be retold.
35. Flowering
The chainsaw roars, it cuts and tears
Through each root, it has no fears
No plant can stand against its might
It's like a storm that clears the night
But there's a plant, so strong and true
Piercing through the ground, anew

The chainsaw tries to cut it down
But fails, it stumbles to the ground
For this plant shall never fall
Its roots too strong, it stands so tall
It's an oxymoron, it's a paradox
An unyielding plant among the rocks
Yet time goes on, the plant grows more
It spreads its leaves and extends its core
And so, the chainsaw comes once more
To trim and cut, until it falls once more
And so, it's like the start again
The chainsaw's roar, the pain, the strain
The plant remains, a symbol of love
Cut down, but always rising above.

37. In the week of silence, the world grows still
As the dark rolls in with fog and dusty chill
The leaves they settle, the birds they hush
All around is quiet, not even a rush
But amidst this calm, a voltra appears
A burst of light that breaks through the fears
The oxymoron of light in the dark
Bringing hope to those who need a spark
For in this week, the world may seem dead
But the voltra reminds us of what lies ahead
A new day will dawn, the fog will lift
And life will continue, as the darkness shifts.
38.
The clock ticks on the wall, a constant reminder
Of the time slipping by, a relentless chider
Through the city streets I rush, seeking an escape
From the ceaseless routine, the endless retape
Each day seems the same, a monotonous blur
As I search for a path, a way to demur
But every turn I take, every street I roam
Leads me back to where I started, a place called home
The city lights flicker, a colorful array
As I wander the streets, searching for a new way
Every loophole I find, every crack in the wall
Leads me to the same destination, trapped in this fall
But still I keep searching, for a way to break free
From this cycle of madness, this unceasing spree
For though the city may bind me, it can't break my will
To find the light in the darkness, to climb the highest hill

39.
A ship that sinks with every step,
My body withers, is slowly crept
Towards the abyss, a darkening hue
As I fade away, into something new.
The captain sees my fate, with grief
As I let go, into the reef
But in my leaving, he finds a place
A paradise, a beautiful space.
In this world, where time is fleet
I reflect on the hundredth beat
Of the hundredth day and year
With memories, ever so dear.
For as the ship sinks, I find new land
And beauty in the captain's hand
And as I fade, another is reborn
A life like mine, to be adorned.
So let the ship sink, let the sea take hold
As I step into a world, so bold
For in every moment, there is beauty to find
And a new home, waiting, so kind.
40. Roundabout of memories
In the middle of the roundabout, a man stood,
Watching cars go by, year after year.
In the tenth month, the memories flood,
Each corner holding a different tear.
Here he stood on the day of his love's death,
Frozen in time, his heart still in pain.
He remembered her smile and her last breath,
And all the moments they would never regain.
Then on the next corner, his wedding day,
A different kind of memory came to play.

He saw her in her dress, walking his way,
And felt the love that would never sway.
But time moves on, as do the cars,
And soon a bus was headed his way.
He saw the faces of those left behind,
And with a single word, he let them all stay:
"Goodbye."
Fly
41. The world spins on, each day a new portal
Opens up, revealing different lives
Of different people, each with their mortal
Journey to live, but some are left to strive.
Upon a doorstep, a small, frail child lay
Forgotten by those who should have loved most,
But the winds of fate did not let him stay
Weak and helpless, for he was meant to boast.
With the years, he grew to be strong and wise,
Those early struggles forging a path true.
And though the world still filled with many lies,
He knew his purpose, what he could pursue.
Through all his strife, he stood with head held high,
His legacy summed up with one word: "Fly."
42. In the river's icy embrace,
A shiver runs through veins, no trace,
Of warmth or solace to be found,
Only the chill, deep and profound.
Each droplet a sharp and biting sting,
Echoes of heartbreak, a frozen fling,
The water, a mirror of love unfulfilled,
Leaving an emptiness, so coldly distilled.
The river's current, swift and strong,
Reflects the anguish, the pain prolonged,

It shocks the body, numbs the soul,
Leaving an icy heart, never made whole.
Yet, amidst the depths of this frigid flow,
Strength emerges from our hearts, we know,
For even in the coldest wintery gaze,
Love can thaw the frost, ignite the blaze.
So let the river rush, let it freeze,
For within this icy heart, the warmth will seize,
And though the cold may linger for a while,
Love's flame will melt it, bring forth a smile.
43. Amidst the sorrow and despair, nature stands,
A testament to resilience, painted by nature's hands.
The trees, resolute in their graceful sway,
Whispering solace, as if to say,
"We have witnessed heartbreak, so profound,
Yet, we grow tall, firmly rooted in the ground.
Our branches reach for heavens, beyond the pain,
For in nature's embrace, healing does reign."
The flowers bloom with vibrant array,
Their petals unfurl, embracing the day.
Though their roots may ache, buried deep,
They rise above, a testament to resilience, they keep.
The gentle breeze, a balm to the soul,
Softly whispers secrets, helping us feel whole.
Carrying the scent of roses and lavender,
It reminds us that healing is always near.
The birds, with their melodic tunes,
Sing of hope beneath the grieving moon.
Their wings beat rhythmically, a metaphor so true,
That life goes on, despite what we've been through.
The sun, with its golden rays, so bright,
Shines on the world, casting away the night.

It warms us, reminds us of brighter days,
When heartbreak's burden begins to erase.
Nature's resistance against the pain,
Teaches us strength, helps us regain,
The courage to heal, the power to mend,
And find solace in the beauty that will transcend.
For in the solace of nature's embrace,
We find renewal, as it reflects our grace.
Through heartbreak's storm, we'll rise above,
Embracing the resilience of nature's love.
44.
In the depths of sorrow's icy grip,
I yearn to go back, to take that fateful trip.
For in my hands lay the letters, unread,
Words of love and longing left unsaid.
Oh, the weight of regret, heavy as stone,
As I sit here, trembling, all alone.
Each word, a dagger plunging deep,
Piercing my soul, refusing to sleep.
Time slips away, like grains of sand,
As the pain of heartbreak takes its stand.
In each letter's lines, a tale untold,
A story of passion, now grown cold.
Oh, how I ache, with every passing breath,
Knowing that I failed to grasp love's depth.
The ink of her words, once vibrant and alive,
Now stains my heart, a painful dive.
The coldness seeps into my very core,
Frostbite of the spirit, forevermore.
For in those letters, the warmth I seek,
Frigid winds howl, as my soul grows weak.
I trace my steps through memories vast,

Searching for reasons, trying to grasp,
How did I not see the signs so clear?
How did I let her love slowly disappear?
But time cannot rewind, the past stands still,
And with each frozen heartbeat, my longing grows uphill.
Yet, amid the pain, a flame flickers within,
A beacon of hope, refusing to rescind.
For even in the depths of endless cold,
A flame of redemption can still unfold.
I'll read those letters now, one by one,
Immerse myself in the love I had shunned.
Though regret lingers, suffocating my soul,
I'll face the heartache, seek to be whole.
For in the chill of heartbreak's dark abyss,
I'll find strength, and from it, eternal bliss.
The notes
Note 1.
In the middle of the roundabout, a man stood,
Watching cars go by, year after year.
In the tenth month, the memories flood,
Each corner holding a different tear.

· · · ·

HERE HE STOOD ON THE day of his love's death,
Frozen in time, his heart still in pain.
He remembered her smile and her last breath,
And all the moments they would never regain.

· · · ·

THEN ON THE NEXT CORNER, his wedding day,
A different kind of memory came to play.
He saw her in her dress, walking his way,

And felt the love that would never sway.

. . . .

BUT TIME MOVES ON, as do the cars,
  And soon a bus was headed his way.
  He saw the faces of those left behind,
  And with a single word, he let them all stay:

. . . .

"GOODBYE."

. . . .

NOTE 2.
  The world spins on, each day a new portal
  Opens up, revealing different lives
  Of different people, each with their mortal
  Journey to live, but some are left to strive.

. . . .

UPON A DOORSTEP, A small, frail child lay
  Forgotten by those who should have loved most,
  But the winds of fate did not let him stay
  Weak and helpless, for he was meant to boast.

. . . .

WITH THE YEARS, HE grew to be strong and wise,
  Those early struggles forging a path true.
  And though the world still filled with many lies,
  He knew his purpose, what he could pursue.

. . . .

THROUGH ALL HIS STRIFE, he stood with head held high,
    His legacy summed up with one word: "Fly."

· · · ·

NOTE 3.
    The sun beats down upon my skin,
    Reflecting memories of where I've been.
    Through heartbreak and highs and lows,
    The sun has seen it all, I suppose.

· · · ·

ITS RAYS ARE WARM AND ever so bright,
    A gentle reminder that everything's alright.
    Though sometimes clouds can get in the way,
    The sun always manages to brighten the day.

· · · ·

BUT EVEN THE SUN MUST eventually set,
    And the mood begins to change, I bet.
    As it drifts away into the horizon,
    A sense of peace and calm starts to dawn.

· · · ·

REDEMPTION IS HERE, a new chance to start,
    And the sun will rise again, playing its part.
    Reflecting the highs and lows of life,
    A constant reminder to embrace the strife.

· · · ·

SO BASK IN THE SUN'S warm embrace,
    Let it shine upon your face.

For even in the darkest of times,
The sun will always rise and shine.

. . . .

NOTE 4.
Life at Its Lowest

. . . .

MY HEART, IT BEATS with a heavy thud,
Reflecting every day that's filled with mud.
Each moment feels like a million years,
Endless suffering, endless tears.

. . . .

THE WEIGHT UPON MY shoulders grows,
As each day comes with new lows.
I try my best to carry on,
But the darkness, it feels so strong.

. . . .

ANOTHER DAY, ANOTHER fight,
Trying to make it through the night.
But hope is something that's hard to find,
When you're struggling to stay alive.

. . . .

I KEEP ON MOVING, THOUGH I'm crushed,
Every step feels like a push and a shove.
Can't seem to escape these endless pains,
Exhausted, isolated, fatigue gains.

. . . .

ONE DAY TURNS INTO another,
    Blurs of gray shade is all I uncover.
    Each one harder than the last,
    Wishing this agony would just pass.

• • • •

GOODBYE AND GOOD LUCK,
    One word, to end this poem so abrupt.
    May tomorrow bring new beginnings,
    And my shattered heart, it stops spinning.

• • • •

NOTE 5.
    A gun, polished and clean,
    Sits on a table, waiting to be seen.
    A symbol of power and might,
    Yet its purpose is simply to fight.

• • • •

IN THE FIRST SHOT, the man's mind is hit,
    His thoughts scatter like a bullet's spit.
    The pros and cons of life appear,
    As he contemplates his doubts and fear.

• • • •

NEXT, THE BULLET PENETRATES his flesh,
    The pain is real, a physical mesh.
    The body's limitations are shown,
    As mortality rears its head, fully grown.

• • • •

FINALLY, THE LAST SHOT is fired,
The man's heart, it leaves him expired.
For all his dreams and aspirations,
Death is the ultimate demonstration.

• • • •

LIFE IS A ROUNDABOUT, a cyclical ride,
Where everyone and everything collide.
Moods soar and plummet like a rollercoaster,
As reality becomes a boisterous host.

• • • •

HAVE FAITH, LOOK BEYOND the veil,
For what's after is more than just a tale.
Embrace the journey, the joy and pain,
For life's experiences are what remain.

• • • •

NOTE 6.
Words on the fridge, a common sight,
A note from here, a thought for there,
Each message a different word,
In a symphony of notes we share.

• • • •

SELF-DOUBT, PAIN, DEPRESSION, hope,
All the words we know so well,
Notes that pass from hand to hand,
Telling stories, hard to tell.

• • • •

LOVE, TRUST, AND A fighting spirit,
    Each note a rallying cry,
    A reminder of our strengths deep down,
    And the reasons we must try.

• • • •

BUT THERE ARE THOSE who have it all,
    Buried in wealth yet still so sad,
    Their hearts weighed heavy with pain,
    A life that isn't what they had.

• • • •

THEN THERE ARE THOSE, so full of joy,
    With nothing to their name,
    A simple life, a pure heart,
    A soul that burned like a flame.

• • • •

ON EACH GRAVE, A SINGLE note,
    A reminder of the end that comes,
    Death is inevitable, they say,
    But its finality still feels like a bomb.

• • • •

AND SO WE LIVE WITH words unsaid,
    Notes never shared with those we love,
    We must cherish each moment we have,
    For it's fleeting, like a dove.

• • • •

THESE NOTES ON THE fridge, a reminder,

Of battles fought and lost and won,
But the notes that I never received,
Were the ones that could have just begun.

. . . .

NOTE 7.
A hill stands tall and proud,
Its peak reaching towards the sky.
A symbol of nature's beauty,
A sight that catches the eye.

. . . .

DEEP WITHIN THIS HILL,
A hole descends, dark and cold,
Growing wider every year,
A story waiting to be told.

. . . .

FOR MANY YEARS IT GREW,
A reminder of pain and sorrow,
And on that fateful day,
It closed, holding secrets to follow.

. . . .

THE NOTES OF LOVE AND loss,
Locked away for all to see,
A heartbreak so raw and real,
A tragedy for all to feel.

. . . .

BUT TIME HAS A FUNNY way,

Of healing wounds we thought may never mend,
And one day, in the spring,
A poppy blooms, bringing a hopeful end.

• • • •

THIS TINY FLOWER, BOLD and bright,
A symbol of new life and growth,
A sign that even in darkness,
There's always a chance for hope.

• • • •

NOTE 8.
A week unlike any other,
When all the world went still,
Silent moments, alone with thoughts,
A space that could almost kill.

• • • •

BUT ON THE WALLS, MESSAGES appeared,
Notes sent with love and care,
Each one marking off the days,
This silence was hard to bear.

• • • •

DAYS AND MONTHS, THEY passed us by,
The notes on the walls grew strong,
But then on one fateful Monday,
Everything disappeared, all wrong.

• • • •

THERE, UPON THE GRAVEDIGGED earth,

Lay a note so stark and dark,
Just one word, a warning clear,
A warning, certainly not for the weak of heart.

. . . .

AND SO WE STAND IN somber thought,
  Wondering what it could all mean,
  But we know we need to stay strong,
  And keep the memories keen.

. . . .

FOR EVEN WHEN THERE'S silence,
  We'll keep our love alive,
  A force that binds us all together,
  And helps us to truly thrive.

. . . .

NOTE 9.
  He looked down at his bed,
  Heart shattered, tears shed.
  A note lay before him,
  Words cutting to the core, so grim.

. . . .

"I LOVE YOU BUT I CANNOT
  Love the idea of dating the monster
  Underneath your skin," she wrote
  His heart sank, his dreams afloat.

. . . .

THE ANNIVERSARY OF their breakup

And here he was, all alone, stuck
With memories that haunt his soul
And the reality that took its toll.

. . . .

GOODBYE, HE WHISPERED,
   As he let go of what they shared.
   It was a painful truth to accept
   But he knew it was time to move ahead.

. . . .

GOOD RIDDANCE, HE BREATHED,
   As he released the pain and sorrow.
   He was done with the heartache
   And was ready for a better tomorrow.

. . . .

NOTE 10.
   Life upon life, a never-ending stream,
   Each day a challenge, full of heartbreaks and pain,
   Pens and papers surround me, a writer's dream,
   But sometimes solace seems so hard to gain.

. . . .

THEN CAME A DAY WHEN a note caught my eye,
   A simple message with three words so pure,
   "I love you," it said, and I couldn't deny
   The warmth it brought, a feeling so secure.

. . . .

THE GIRL WHO WROTE it, she stole my heart,

And showed me love, a different kind of art.
I realized then that life is not just strife,
That love exists, and it can change your life.

. . . .

SO NOW I WRITE WITH a new sense of grace,
With her by my side, my heart's a better place.

. . . .

NOTE 11.
Every poem ever made is a journey to behold
Through the lines and stanzas, stories are told
From heartbreaks and love to battles won and lost
Each poem a treasure, a story at its best.

. . . .

AS TIME PASSES BY, the weight of words grows tall
A block of walls, with notes scattered, some big and small.
But amidst it all, there's a shining note that glows
And as it opens up, the beauty of poetry flows.

. . . .

IN THAT NOTE LIES THE hope and dreams of everyone we adore
A shining apple, full of stories, we can't ignore
For it's the essence of passion, the spark that ignites the fire
And with every word we write, our love for it grows higher.

. . . .

AS WE COME TO THE END of the ever after
And the journey of poetry takes its final chapter
We'll treasure every poem, every word we ever wrote

As it represents the love and dreams of everyone we ever loved and hoped.

· · · ·

NOTE 12.

    From yonder hill, I see you running wild,
    Your voice, a joyful tune to reach my ear,
    My heart, with love and passion, is beguiled,
    As you approach, my soul begins to cheer.

· · · ·

YOUR EYES, A WINDOW to your loving soul,
    Reflecting all the light within your heart,
    Your laughter makes my heart feel truly whole,
    And from your love, I vow never to part.

· · · ·

FOR IN YOUR EYES, I see a world of bliss,
    A world where love and joy forever reign,
    Where every single moment filled with kiss
    And all the sorrows, forever slain.

· · · ·

SO, TO THE LOVE THAT makes my heart complete,
    Your presence, my love, makes my heart beat!

· · · ·

ONE WORD ENDING: FOREVER.

· · · ·

NOTE 13.

. . . .

LIFE ITSELF

. . . .

FROM THE FIRST BREATH that graced our lungs,
   To the last gasp that whispered goodbye,
   Life unfolds, a tapestry of moments,
   An ever-changing melody in the sky.

. . . .

WITH EACH STEP WE TAKE upon this earth,
   Through joys and sorrows, we learn and grow,
   And as we journey closer to the end,
   A new understanding begins to flow.

. . . .

THE ENDINGS COME AS gentle whispers,
   Embraced with wisdom, acceptance adorns,
   For life's sweet essence lies not in length,
   But in how gracefully it is adorned.

. . . .

LIKE THE SUN THAT SETS upon the horizon,
   Casting hues of gold and purple hue,
   We find solace in the fading light,
   As endings bring new beginnings through.

. . . .

SO LET US SAVOR THE dance of breath,
   From the first inhale to the final sigh,
   For in acceptance, we find a freedom,

To embrace life's fullness, even as we say goodbye.

• • • •

NOTE 14.

• • • •

BIRTH OF POETRY

• • • •

IN THE BIRTH OF DUSK, where light descends,
    Emerges the start, the beginning of an end,
    Whence fate and time intertwine their threads,
    A solemn finale to all that man comprehends.

• • • •

AS THE SUN SETS, CASTING shadows ablaze,
    A tapestry woven in nature's subtle ways,
    The symphony of existence reaches its crescendo,
    Echoing through realms beyond what we can show.

• • • •

ONCE VIBRANT DREAMS, now mere echoes of the past,
    Permeating the ether, fading ever so fast,
    Memories wane like flickering candle flame,
    In this twilight hour, whence silence lays claim.

• • • •

THE DENOUEMENT UNFOLDS, a cosmic ballet,
    Stars dance in celestial array,
    Galaxies collide, bound by celestial ties,
    Unveiling truth beneath celestial skies.

. . . .

A REQUIEM ECHOES IN the universe's expanse,
A lamentation for what once had a chance,
The melody of life, now a distant refrain,
As the orchestra reaches its final refrain.

. . . .

THE COSMOS UNRAVELS, in cosmic artistry,
A grand finale, birthed from eternity,
The symphony of creation reaches its last note,
And all that was known begins to demote.

. . . .

WITH THE LAST STROKE of destiny's brush,
Reality shatters, in a deafening hush,
Beyond the edge, a new realm unfolds,
Where stories untold, the universe molds.

. . . .

IN THE DEPTHS OF DARKNESS, a spark ignites,
A seed of creation amidst infinite nights,
From the ashes of the known, a genesis anew,
The cyclical dance of life begins its debut.

. . . .

SO FEAR NOT, DEAR SOUL, as the end draws near,
For with every finale, new beginnings appear,
In the tapestry of existence, as it unravels and mends,
A wondrous journey awaits, where a new story transcends.

. . . .

NOTE 15.

. . . .

HER EVERY HER

. . . .

IN THE OPAQUE DEPTHS of memory's vast sea,
   I found fragments of a love story,
   With a melody that once held serenity.

. . . .

SHE, AN ENIGMA DRAPED in twilight's grasp, *
   A tableau of beauty, fierce and wild,
   Each breath a whisper, each step beguiled.

. . . .

HER LAUGHTER, A SYMPHONY of stolen mirth, *
   A radiant sunbeam piercing through the mist,
   Her presence a balm, a gentle, sweet twist.

. . . .

BUT OH, THE SHADOWS that danced upon her heart, *
   Thoughts consumed by gnawing regret,
   Whispers that promised endless torment.

. . . .

IN HER SECRET MOMENTS, she grappled with pain, *
   A storm raging within, desperate and vile,
   Oh, how she detested the mask she wore with a smile.

. . . .

THE WORLD SAW PERFECTION, an ethereal guise, *
But she, in the depths of her being, despised,
A gallery of self-loathing she disguised.

. . . .

HER DELICATE FAÇADE hid a tempestuous curse, *
Fingers tracing scars buried deep within,
A symphony of self-hate, an agonized din.

. . . .

YET, IN THE CHAOS OF her sorrowful soul, *
She was a portrait of vibrant hues,
The embodiment of love she couldn't refuse.

. . . .

SO, LET NOT HATRED consume my every word, *
For her struggle was not for me to define,
But hers alone, a battle against malign.

. . . .

IN THE TAPESTRY OF her complex existence, *
I glimpsed both darkness and shimmering light,
And in her absence, I send wishes of respite.

. . . .

MAY SHE FIND SOLACE in self-love's embrace, *
And shed the burden of her inner strife,
To paint new canvases, abundant with life.

. . . .

FOR SHE, MY EX, FOREVER intertwined,

With a mosaic of memories, sacred and kind,
A testament of love, despite the pain we find.

. . . .

NOTE 16.

. . . .

61 LEAFS
Bright orange leafs dance,
Seasons changing, nature's art,
Late night drives, love's warmth.

. . . .

61'S WINDING,
Whispers of memories past,
Shared moments now lost.

. . . .

FALL'S HUES EMBRACE us,
As bittersweet sorrow lingers,
Love's touch now distant.

. . . .

YET, IN TENDER DREAMS,
Leafs on trees and love unfold,
Moments once cherished.

. . . .

NOTE 17.

. . . .

THE REVOLUTION OF THE dreams

. . . .

IN THE REALM OF THOUGHTS and dreams, I write,
A revolution brewing in my mind's sphere,
Where visions flourish, taking flight at night.

. . . .

WITHIN MY WORDS, THE battles come alive,
For the pen's mightier than the sword's fierce glare,
In the realm of thoughts and dreams, I write.

. . . .

IDEAS SPROUT, UNLEASH their power to ignite,
With ink as my weapon, I make aware,
Where visions flourish, taking flight at night.

. . . .

A SYMPHONY OF WORDS, a rebel's plight,
Against injustice, a cause I hold dear,
In the realm of thoughts and dreams, I write.

. . . .

YET NOT ALONE IN THIS creative fight,
For comrades stand, their support sincere,
Where visions flourish, taking flight at night.

. . . .

TOGETHER WE STRIVE to change the wrongs to right,
With revolution's anthem ringing clear,
In the realm of thoughts and dreams, I write,

Where visions flourish, taking flight at night.

Note 18.

The others

In realms unknown, the other side unveiled,
Where words entangle, jumbled and assailed.
The tapestry of thoughts, in disarray,
Mixed fragments blend, a chaotic display.

• • • •

A DANCE OF LETTERS, twisted and confused,
Vivid hues of language, now bemused.
Like tangled vines, the meaning seeks release,
Unraveled lines, a challenge to appease.

• • • •

FOR IN THIS MAZE, THE end of the end,
Fragile pages falter and descend.
A riddle forged, where clarity is lost,
Each word entwined, an intricate exhaust.

• • • •

OH, THE OTHER EVERYTHING, perplexing maze,
Where syntax bleeds, and syntax betrays.
Like puzzle pieces scrambled in the fray,
The final chapter crumbles to dismay.

• • • •

YET SOMEHOW, IN THIS muddled disarray,
A glimmer, faint, persists through the dismay.
The reader's mind, a beacon in the dark,
Unveiling truths, emerging like a spark.

• • • •

SO FEAR NOT, FRIEND, the jumbled book's intent,

For in the chaos, brilliance may be sent.
Grasp each mixed word, let meaning intertwine,
The end of the end, a gateway to divine.

. . . .

NOTE 19.
In the darkness of the room, I lie in bed,
Shadows dance, a silent symphony in my head.
Lost in the midnight's silky embrace,
Recalling the first date, our hearts' gentle trace.

. . . .

A BEAM OF MOONLIGHT whispers on the wall,
Revealing the memories that I recall.
A note she gave me, etched with love's gentle art,
"I love you," it said, eternally bound to my heart.

. . . .

BENEATH THE COVERS, cocooned in warmth and grace,
I see her face in every shadow's embrace.
Her laughter echoes, filling the silent air,
As I lay, captivated by the love we share.

. . . .

AND THOUGH TIME MAY pass, and darkness may reside,
In my dreams, her love forever shall abide.
For through the shadows, her light will always shine,
A reminder that true love is beautifully divine.

. . . .

VERSE:

In the embrace of shadows, love's sweet truth,
Eternal whispers in the dark, I speak of you.

· · · ·

NOTE 20.
In a hotel of moments, spinning rooms abound,
Wandering souls, lost, seeking what can't be found.
With each creaking step, uncertainty unfurls,
And in the midst, a number, two-nine-nine, it swirls.

· · · ·

A GLIMPSE OF THE PAST, a journey to the year,
Two-thousand and ninety-nine, love's frontier.
Together we ventured, in a world yet unknown,
Our future unfurling, seeds of hope sown.

· · · ·

IN ROOM TWO-OH-NINE-nine, our dreams took flight,
Hand in hand, we walked, bathed in love's pure light.
The tapestry of time, a tapestry so grand,
We witnessed our destiny, hand in hand.

· · · ·

BUT FATE HAS ITS WAY, it's a merciless beast,
As love's majestic dance took a tragic release.
Our laughter turned hollow, as the walls crashed down,
The bittersweet memory, forever to be bound.

· · · ·

ROOMS SPINNING, MEMORIES walking, oh, what a sight,
From two-oh-nine-nine to two-nine-nine, our plight.

In echoes of the past, we find solace and pain,
Yet through it all, love's fire forever shall remain.

. . . .

NOTE 21.
In room two-nine-nine, shattered and worn,
A haven of despair, its walls forlorn.
The structure, once sturdy, now crumbled with strife,
A reflection of a fractured, weary life.

. . . .

LINES BREAK, LIKE CRACKS upon fragile glass,
Symbolic fractures of a soul's trespass.
Rhyme disintegrates, as darkness takes its hold,
An unraveling tale, once bright, now grown cold.

. . . .

STANZAS CRUMBLE, MIRRORING the room's decay,
Revealing the agony, concealed away.
Each syllable, laden with a weight so deep,
A sorrowful secret, no longer to keep.

. . . .

WITH EACH VERSE, A piece of hope follows suit,
Yet, overshadowed by melancholy's pursuit.
The depth of the ending, a profound descent,
A melancholic resonance, in sorrow, we're sent.

. . . .

FOR BENEATH THE RUINED shell of room two-nine-nine,
Lies an ache so profound, an anguish, divine.

In its wreckage, a metaphor, plain to perceive,
The depth of a heartache that refuses to leave.

· · · ·

SO LET THE POEM'S STRUCTURE reflect the pain,
A tumultuous journey with little to gain.
In the end, a resonating truth we find,
That beauty can arise from a wreckage of mind.

· · · ·

NOTE 22.
In a realm where wonders dwell, upon a hill of mystic hue,
There glistens a tapestry of gems, on sky's canvas, born anew.
For high above, where dreams take flight, rare treasures shimmer bright,
A celestial dance in ethereal haze, a sight to ignite pure delight.

· · · ·

OH, THE HILL WHERE rare gems reside, suspended in celestial embrace,
Their brilliance strewn across the air, a celestial treasure trove to chase.
Each gem a universe in itself, a kaleidoscope of vibrant hues,
Emerald whispers, sapphire laughter, amethyst secrets woven true.

· · · ·

AS THE DAYS UNFOLD, the hill does shrink, like a page too quickly turned,
Perched upon its shrinking crest, a people whose hearts have learned,
To cherish beauty with gentle love, to honor each precious stone,
For they are linked, their fates entwined, in this dwindling celestial zone.

• • • •

THEIR LIVES A FRAGILE tapestry, woven with care and tender grace,
For as the hill recedes from sight, they seek solace in this sacred space.
Gathered in unity, like petals of a fleeting bloom, they thrive,
Embracing the gems as their own, keeping them alive.

• • • •

EACH DWELLER HOLDS a gem of worth, within their very soul,
A reflection of the hill, a shimmering essence that makes them whole.
With every breath, they revere the beauty lingering in the air,
For the hill may fade, but its spirit will forever be theirs to bear.

• • • •

OH, THE HILL WHERE rare gems reside, shining brighter than all the rest,
It may diminish in its grandeur, yet its luster will never truly be suppressed.
For within the hearts of those who dwell, its magic will forever ignite,
A connection to celestial wonders, a love that burns eternally bright.

• • • •

SO LET US LEARN FROM the hill and its gems, both rare and divine,
To cherish the fading moments, to savor the beauty that intertwines.
For even as the hill becomes a memory, in our hearts it remains,
A testament to the power of love, where its radiant light forever reigns.

• • • •

NOTE 23.

• • • •

IN THE EMBRACE OF NATURE'S rocky arms, the mountains soar high,
Their ancient peaks stand tall, caressed by the endless sky.
They harbor secrets deep within, stories whispered by the wind,
As water weaves its way, through canyons carved by time.

• • • •

A SYMPHONY OF WHISPERS, the flowing stream sings its song,
Cascading over mossy rocks, where solitude thrives, serene and strong.
Through valleys and meadows, it dances with effortless grace,
Cleansing the land with every ripple, a tranquil and sacred chase.

• • • •

YET HIDDEN WITHIN THESE wonders lies a room named 299,
A chamber of enigmas, where the unknown intertwines.
Behind its silent door, mysteries unfold, veiled in shadows deep,
Whispers echo through its halls, secrets that time longs to keep.

• • • •

A KEYHOLE HOLDS THE tales of those who've come and gone,
Rooms within a room, secrets conjoined, like lyrics to a forgotten song.
Curiosity beckons from the threshold, drawing us near,
To unravel the hidden mysteries, to confront the unknown without fear.

• • • •

IN ROOM 299, WHERE time suspends its ceaseless flow,
Imagination dances, as the mysteries continue to grow.

Through corridors of uncertainty and shadows cast askew,
We venture forth, captivated by the secrets room 299 ensues.

• • • •

FOR LIKE THE MOUNTAINS that caress the sky, and the water's gentle rinse,
    Mysteries hold a certain allure, akin to nature's timeless brilliance.
    They beckon us to explore the depths, to wander and to seek,
    In the realm of the unknown, where answers and truths may speak.

• • • •

SO LET US EMBRACE THE mountains and the flowing water's song,
    As we venture into Room 299, a place where secrets belong.
    For in those hidden whispers, there lies a chance to discover,
    That the greatest mystery of all, is the vastness of our own spirit's cover.

Don't miss out!

Visit the website below and you can sign up to receive emails whenever KERNAN publishes a new book. There's no charge and no obligation.

https://books2read.com/r/B-A-ITHAB-YDRNC

BOOKS 2 READ

Connecting independent readers to independent writers.

About the Author

My names Jacob I'm 15 year years old a young writer but seen experience throughout my life my 9 part book series reflects all of it from the soul of me

www.ingramcontent.com/pod-product-compliance
Lightning Source LLC
Chambersburg PA
CBHW031500130726
47989CB00003B/1470